C000067204

BOTH
PUBLISHING

Published in 2021 by BOTH Publishing.

The author asserts their moral right to be identified as the author of their work, in accordance with the Copyright, Designs and Patents Act, 1988.

A CIP catalogue record of this book is available from the British Library.

ISBN - 978-1-913603-06-9
eBook available - ISBN - 978-1-913603-07-6

Printed in the UK by TJ Books Limited.
Distributed by BOTH Publishing.

Cover design by Chrissey Harrison and Alistair Sims. Typeset by Chrissey Harrison.

Part of the Dyslexic Friendly Quick Reads Series.

www.booksonthehill.co.uk

ULTRASOUND SHADOW

Thana Niveau

Other dyslexic friendly quick read titles from BOTH publishing

The House on the Old Cliffs

The Clockwork Eyeball

Anchor Point

At Midnight I Will Steal Your Soul

The Breath

Sherlock Holmes and the
Four Kings of Sweden

The Man Who Would Be King

Ultrasound

Shadow

Molly stared at the little plastic wand, her eyes fixed on the twin pink stripes in their tiny adjacent windows. She checked the directions again. She must have read them wrong the first time. The second time too. Or maybe she'd done the test wrong. Maybe there was some other way you were meant to wee on the little stick. It wouldn't be the first time she'd screwed up something so simple.

But no. The directions were as plain as could be and the photograph on

1

the box left no room for interpretation. A pink line in each window meant PREGNANT. It was unequivocal. It was true. Fuck.

She threw the whole lot into the bin and snatched up her phone. *You were right,* she texted to Alice. Her friend had spotted the signs before Molly had even known there were any. She often felt ill in the morning, usually due to overindulgence the night before. But Alice had sussed that it was more than just a string of hangovers.

"You look pale," she'd said. "Pasty even."

"Thanks."

"Seriously, it's just how Carly looked when she got pregnant. Don't you remember?"

Molly did, vaguely. What she remembered most about Carly was the reckless flurry of partying the three had done, living it up as much as they could before the mum-to-be started to show. They'd bade their friend's slim figure farewell on a weekend break to Tenerife, where Alice mislaid their passports and they had to stay an extra night, to no one's chagrin. It was an amazing holiday and Molly remembered her childish hope that it would change Carly's mind about having the baby.

But it was not to be. When the girls returned to Bristol, Carly proposed to her boyfriend and gradually drifted away. Marriage and motherhood had broken up the trio.

Molly's phone bleeped with a response from Alice. *Dinner?*

Pizza, she texted back. *And wine. LOTS of wine.*

Molly Landor was only thirty-three. And while she'd always imagined having kids someday, she *had* rather hoped it would be by choice and not by accident.

She was careful. Most of the time. But, she supposed, it only took one mistake. And there had been a lot of guys. A lot of casual encounters she couldn't even remember. There was no telling who the father might be. The drummer in that band she and Alice had gone to see three weeks ago? The Russian guy who'd asked her for directions to the cathedral? Possibly even

Danny, her fuck-buddy in London. Hell, it could be *anyone.*

"Hey kiddo," Alice said, giving her friend the gentlest of hugs.

"It's not cancer," Molly grumbled, "I'm just pregnant." She squeezed Alice fiercely, suddenly wishing that their one-off drunken fumble at uni had made her a lesbian. Then she wouldn't be in this predicament. Girls couldn't get each other knocked up.

The waiter led them to a table by the window and Molly sank into her chair with a sigh. She ordered a bottle of pinot grigio and stared forlornly out the window for a long time. She was reluctant to say the words aloud, superstitiously afraid it would mark the point of no return.

"Well," she said at last, "you were right."

Alice clasped Molly's hands across the table. "What are you going to do?"

Molly shook her head. "I don't know. I mean, now that I *know*, it's not so easy. I always thought if I wasn't ready, I'd just get it hoovered out, you know? But now I'm not sure."

"You mean you want to keep it?"

"I don't know. That's the weird thing. I don't suddenly feel all broody and maternal but I also don't feel like it's the worst thing in the world. I was gutted when I saw the test result, but just in the past couple of hours things have changed. So much has gone through my head. Maybe it's a sign. Or something.

Oh, I just don't know!"

The waiter arrived with their wine and Molly gulped half her glass before he had even finished pouring Alice's.

"Hey, wait for me," Alice laughed. "I'm not sure if it's something to toast or not, but it sounds as if you don't know either, so what the hell." She raised her glass and clinked it against Molly's. "Here's to… well, a new life."

Molly smiled and finished her glass in two swallows. She pulled the bottle out of its ice bucket and topped it up.

Alice raised an eyebrow and Molly held up her hand. "Don't start. This kid ambushed me and if I keep it, it's gonna take over my whole life. The least it can do is let me enjoy some wine with my best friend."

"While you decide its fate."

"Yeah. Fate. Funny thing, that."

"I thought you were an atheist."

Molly shrugged. "Who knows? Anything's possible. I mean, we never thought Carly would go through with it, did we?"

"Still can't believe that," Alice said, shaking her head. She caught the waiter's eye and waved her menu. "That was three years and two kids ago and the last time I saw her she was making noises about wanting another one."

An image came to Molly of herself several years down the line. Her face worn and haggard, her complexion sallow, her lustrous auburn hair limp and stringy. A litter of rugrats clustering around her, tugging at the frumpy skirts and oversized T-shirts she'd have taken to wearing. She shuddered and turned to the waiter, who was asking if he could take their order. He was probably ten years her junior. Tall and wiry, with spiky surfer hair and a Polish accent. Gorgeous. She suddenly felt like an old maid and she looked down at the menu so she wouldn't have to meet his beautiful eyes.

She heard Alice order a Caesar salad, which made her stomach rumble in protest. She'd only been technically pregnant for a couple of hours and already she felt like she was eating for two. But what the hell, she was drowning her sorrows today. Self-medicating to treat the shock. And afterwards she intended to treat herself to as much chocolate as she could stand.

"Can I have a pizza?" she asked, realising she hadn't even looked at the choices on the menu.

"Certainly, miss. Which one?"

She flinched at "miss". Had the seed within her suddenly aged her horribly? Alice patted her hand, empathic as always. Only a girlfriend would understand. Molly faced the waiter bravely, trying to block out the image of ordering plain cheese pizzas for a child's unsophisticated palate, mopping tomato sauce off a toddler's face ... Oh, but even before any of that, the horror of the actual *birth*!

"I want lots of meat and lots of chilies. Anchovies too if you have them. Onions. Olives. Everything."

He smiled as he wrote it down, a friendly, innocent smile, oblivious to her distress. "Everything," he repeated. Then he clicked his ballpoint pen and tucked it into his shirt pocket before heading off to the kitchen.

Molly stared out the window. She watched as several people went past and it wasn't long before a woman appeared with a pushchair. Her child was far too old for it, but presumably it was easier than carrying him. Especially as he was in the throes of a violent tantrum. His chubby little legs kicked in clumsy fury and Molly caught sight of his angry red face as the woman went past, looking sad and defeated. Molly turned away, her eyes blurring with tears.

"I don't want it," she said in a shaky voice.

Alice held her hands and offered her a sympathetic smile. "You don't have to decide right now, sweetie. It's a massive decision and you're still reeling from the shock of finding out."

"What if it's horrible? What if it grows up to hate me? What if I hate *it*?"

"Shhhh. There's just as much chance of the opposite, you know. Not all kids are like that one." She jerked her chin towards the window.

"I don't even know how long ago it was," she said, suddenly feeling afraid. "What if it's too late to do anything?"

Alice refilled Molly's glass and pushed the wine towards her. "Calm down. It's only been a few weeks at most. You must know when your last period was."

"Yeah, you're right," Molly said, taking a grateful swallow of wine. "Of course. I couldn't wear the pearl grey dress to the concert that night because I was afraid I'd bleed on it. I remember now. That was – what? Six weeks ago? Two months?"

Alice nodded. "I'm sure it was last month that you started looking so ill. Are you ready for the big question?"

"Fire away."

"Any idea who the father is?"

"I could probably narrow it down to five or six suspects."

Alice's eyes widened. Then she succumbed to laughter. "You total slut."

Molly lifted her glass and grinned. "Hey, they were all first-rate. I don't shag just *anyone*. The kid would have some great genes."

"But hopefully more self-control than its mother."

"Babies have self-control? That's news to me."

She was surprised to find herself remembering fondly the first time she'd ever held a baby. Twelve at the time, Molly had been terrified that she might drop it. It was her cousin's child, a little girl with the princessy name "Aurora". It seemed a million years ago. The tiny blue-eyed creature would be grown now.

Molly realised with a start that she was gently stroking her abdomen and she stopped, hoping Alice hadn't noticed. But her friend was looking towards the kitchen.

The wine had mellowed her considerably and she sat back in her chair, musing. She liked children, but she also cherished her freedom. And her looks. She made a good living as co-manager of a pub so she could certainly afford a child. But did she want to be one of those single mums who had to struggle with schools and child-minders and dating men reluctant to inherit someone else's offspring? What were the alternatives?

Despite her boast to Alice, she couldn't vouch for the breeding stock of anyone. She wouldn't have slept with someone she wasn't attracted to, but sex appeal was no guarantee of health – physical or mental. And even if he was in perfect shape, what if their personalities weren't a fit for marriage? Did she even *want* to be married?

Alice pushed a penny across the table, her eyebrows raised.

"Sorry," Molly said, blushing. "Just sniffing out the territory. Wife versus single mum. Easy decisions like that."

Alice wrinkled her nose. "You're not the marrying kind," she said without hesitation.

"You know me so well." Molly laughed. "I suppose if I'm brutally honest with myself, I'm afraid of finding out who the father is either way. What if I fall in love with him and we get married and then wind up hating each other and resenting the child that forced us together?"

"Hey, there's no law that says you have to get married. Things have changed since the Fifties."

"Yeah, but don't I owe it to the kid to at least let him know his father? Do men have any say in whether a woman has their kid or not? What if *he* wants it and I don't?"

"I think," Alice said, pouring the last of the wine into their glasses, "that this is not the kind of thing you can bash out a quick solution to over dinner. Lock yourself away for a few days and go over all the possibilities. Make some lists.

Sleep on it. *Then* you can start to think about how you want to alter your life and how much."

Molly nodded at her friend's advice. "I know, I know. I'm too impatient." She picked up her glass and held it aloft. "To wise words from wise friends."

Grinning, Alice touched her glass to Molly's. "I don't know about the wise bit but you can certainly count on my friendship. Hell, I'll even watch the kid for you occasionally. If you decide to keep it."

)

Molly returned to her flat that night feeling well fed but only a little drunk. She'd wanted more wine but Alice had begged off, saying she had to be up early and would rather not stagger into work with a blinding hangover. Fair enough; Molly had plenty of booze at home if she needed it.

As she brushed her teeth she couldn't help glancing down at the bin. The white plastic wand was sticking up from the nest of cotton balls and makeup remover wipes. As though either mocking or challenging her. She nudged it out of sight with her foot.

Afterwards she sat at her computer, her fingers poised over the keyboard. The empty search box awaited her queries but she couldn't bring herself to type any of the words that would make her situation even more concrete. She wasn't ready to read about the awful symptoms she could expect from her condition. Nor was she eager to find out exactly what was involved in an abortion. She closed the browser, deciding that for now ignorance was bliss.

Sleep didn't come easily. She tossed and turned, sweating in spite of the chill. She couldn't relax, couldn't get comfortable. The thriller she'd been engrossed in every night couldn't hold her attention now and she snapped the book shut and returned it to the nightstand.

When she ran out of distractions, her thoughts turned to the baby. It was such a tiny thing but it would soon take over her entire world. For the rest of her life it would be central to all her thoughts and decisions. It would consume her, swallow her identity, her independence. But was that really such a bad thing? Wasn't that just the natural way of things, of life?

She closed her eyes and imagined herself communing with the embryo. She visualised her thoughts as strands of light, searching within for a presence. For several minutes she strained her mind to connect. *You're a part of me*, she thought. *What do you want me to do?*

Nothing answered. Feeling a little silly, but at last sleepy, she rolled onto her side and closed her eyes.

)

Her head was throbbing when she woke up and she fought back the nausea she now knew to be morning sickness. She rang Mark at home and told him she wouldn't be around to help with the pub for the next couple of weeks. Family emergency, she said. Not exactly a lie.

She spent her self-imposed exile trying to get her head together. She did the relevant Web searches, forced herself to look at terrifying images and read detailed accounts of the horror and beauty of childbirth. Every time she felt herself begin to warm to the idea she encountered another reason not to go through with it. Going with her gut reaction wasn't an option, as she was truly in two minds.

She considered, then decided against, resuming contact with Carly. A happy family woman could hardly be objective.

Alice checked in with her from time to time and listened patiently to her rants and fears and speculation, but she was careful not to offer advice one way or another. However much she wanted to avoid making the decision, the hard cold truth was that it was Molly's decision alone.

Then one night the baby spoke to her.

It was more a telepathic feeling than an actual voice, but there was no mistaking the message. It wanted life. Molly's eyes filled with tears and she placed her hands on her abdomen.

"Are you sure you want *me*?" she whispered, confronting her greatest insecurity.

All at once she felt flooded with

warmth, then with a hunger so overpowering it made her dizzy. It was a strange, alien desire, originating not from her but from the *other*. Her insides clenched as though the creature within were grasping the wet walls encircling it with tiny claws, demanding to stay.

Molly hissed at the sudden pain and then she took a deep breath, assimilating it. She knew that feeling. It was the lust for survival possessed by all creatures. Pure selfish animal need. A slow smile began to spread across her features. "OK," she said, "I understand."

The cramp eased off and she lay back, gazing through the window at the shadows drifting past the moon. Its bright face beamed as though sharing a secret with her and her unborn child.

"I love you," she told the baby without a trace of self-consciousness. "I can't wait to meet you."

)

Alice was delighted with the news.

"Oh Molly, that's wonderful! I'm really happy for you. I think you'll be a great mum."

"And you'll be a great auntie," Molly said.

"I warn you – I'm going to spoil your brat rotten. Have you thought about names yet?"

Molly nodded and sipped her tea. "I've thought."

"And?"

"He'll tell me when the time comes."

Alice blinked. "He? You mean the father? But I thought you weren't—"

"No. The baby."

Several seconds passed before Alice spoke. "How do you know it's a boy?"

"He told me," Molly said simply.

Alice looked mystified. "Listen, I don't know a lot about these things, but I don't think babies even have a gender until you're about halfway along."

Molly smiled. It was her new smile, a strange and serene expression that made her feel like a creature with a purpose. She'd been admiring it in the mirror each morning since the night of the first contact. It was the moon's gift to her. "He told me," she repeated.

With a baffled shake of her head Alice downed the last of her coffee. "Whatever you say. But you'd better have a backup plan just in case. Have you been to your GP yet?"

"Why do I need to see a doctor?" Molly asked. "I know I'm pregnant."

"Well, you want to check it's healthy, don't you?"

"I know he is."

Alice frowned again and chewed her lip. "But don't you want to make sure? I mean, there are all kinds of things that can go wrong inside and you'd have no way of knowing."

"There's nothing wrong with my baby," Molly said sharply, "however much you might like to think there is."

Hurt flickered in Alice's face and she sat back in her chair as though Molly had slapped her. "I'm just trying to help," she said at last. "There's no need to bite my head off."

"Just trying to help," Molly said with a sneer. "Just jealous is what you are."

"*What?* Molly, what the hell are you talking about?"

"Oh, don't play sweet and stupid with me. I know what you're trying to do and it won't work."

Alice's mouth fell open in an expression of shock that made Molly suddenly despise her.

"There are things you just can't understand unless you're where I am."

Alice's eyes flashed. "Oh, I see. The

whole 'Sacred Mother' thing. You're part of the elite and we the common and childless are too far beneath you to even be worth your time."

Molly raised her eyebrows, an expression that said *Yes, and?*

Alice's chair screeched as she pushed it back violently. "Well, you know where to find me if you ever climb down off your high horse and want your friend back. Thanks for the coffee. And the news. Congratulations. I guess."

Molly stared after her as she flounced out of the café. Then she lowered her gaze to her belly, where her tiny son was floating within. She felt a twinge of anger from there and she stroked the growing bulge.

"There, there," she said softly. "We don't need her. We don't need anyone. We have each other."

Deep inside her the baby stirred, then was calm again.

)

Over the next few weeks Molly began doing what she supposed women did when they were expecting. She cleared out the box room with an eye towards turning it into a nursery.

She went shopping – alone – for the things she thought a baby would need. Shop girls chirpily asked her when she was due but Molly could only guess. Occasional busybodies told her she ought to find out but she found herself bristling at any assistance and eventually she restricted her shopping to the Net.

She returned to work but it soon became clear that she was more of a liability than an asset. She was impatient and snappy with customers and one night she so offended a regular that he stormed out with the promise that he was taking his business down the road where it would be appreciated. Mark gently asked if she wanted to start her maternity leave early.

"Oh, he'll be back," Molly said with a dismissive wave of her hand. "He's been coming here for years."

Mark was unconvinced. "Molly, you've changed."

"Of course I've changed. I'm

pregnant!"

But his expression darkened. "I've got a wife and two kids of my own. I know what pregnant women are like."

"What's that supposed to mean?"

"Just that something's not right. These mood swings, the way you lash out sometimes – it's not like you at all."

The baby twitched and she narrowed her eyes at Mark. "You think there's something wrong with me, is that it? First Alice and now you. Some friends I have."

Her tone was so menacing that he actually took a step back. Unbelievable; he was afraid of her! She could smell his sweat, see the slight widening of his eyes as she pushed her face close to his.

She knew what he was thinking as clearly as if he had spoken.

"Insane?" she asked with mock astonishment. "Who is – me or the baby?"

Mark's eyes widened even more and he shook his head as he backed further away. "I don't think you're well, Molly. You need to see somebody."

He was choosing his words carefully, terrified of angering her, of setting her off. And now that he knew she was in his head he was trying to block his thoughts. It only excited her more.

She smiled sweetly. "Somebody?"

"A doctor," he said, choking out the word.

"Why would I want to do that when

I've never felt better in my life?"

She turned her head enough to catch her reflection in the mirror over the bar. The woman she saw looked radiant. There was an energy there, a potency she'd never felt before. Perhaps that was the "glow" she'd heard that pregnant women were supposed to have.

She looked back at Mark, at his balding head, his mid-life paunch. He reeked of cowardice, of ignorance and stifling banality. He wasn't worth the fury she felt churning inside her.

The customers at the bar were watching the silent showdown with varying degrees of anxiety and interest. The old man on the end fancied her; she could smell his vile lust. And the young couple next to him were wondering if they were about to see a pregnant woman in a pub brawl.

She smiled at the secret knowledge she had of these people. None of them were worth her time.

She reached into her pocket and Mark flinched as though expecting a weapon. But she only withdrew the pub keys. She placed them on the bar, turned and left without a word.

❧

When the first cramp hit, Molly sat up in bed and screamed, clutching her belly. The pain subsided gradually and then another jolt seized her, this one even worse. It felt as though her insides had been filled with fishhooks, their vicious barbs gouging and tearing at the soft lining of her womb.

She couldn't possibly be in labour. It had only been three months, tops. As another wave of pain consumed her she realised with dawning horror what must be happening. She was miscarrying.

Far worse than the pain was the overwhelming sense of anguish, the thought that the bond she had established over the long weeks should now be broken, so suddenly, so violently.

"Stay," she hissed, grimacing as the waves of torment racked her body. "Don't leave me."

The baby had often hurt her, thrashing

inside her like a caged beast. But while his movements were usually of frustration and even rage at his captivity, she knew this time that his struggles were borne of pain. Terrible, terrible pain. He'd been acting strangely all day, writhing and twitching as though in anticipation of this. And Molly had been on edge along with him, sensing an extreme anxiety that bordered on madness.

She'd tried to soothe him with her mind, sending him all the positive feelings she could, but she hadn't been able to break through the suffering to reach him. He was truly in his own little world.

Blinded by tears, she gritted her teeth and tried desperately to focus her mind, to get on top of the spasms so she could save her son. She groped her way to the phone and punched 999. "Help," she gasped. "I'm losing my baby!"

The girl on the other end of the line was talking, trying to get more information, but all Molly could hear was screaming – her own or the baby's, she didn't know which. The sound reverberated throughout her whole body, consuming her. A wail of pure agony that seemed to last for hours.

And then, as suddenly as it had begun, the pain stopped. Molly held her breath, bracing for another contraction. But it never came.

She peered down at herself, amazed and relieved to see that she was whole. There was no rush of blood from beneath her nightgown, no sense that the physical bond between them had been broken. Her baby was alive. Indeed, if anything he felt more alive than ever. He pawed at the tender walls of his prison, but the terrible episode seemed to be over. He was content now, and so was she.

She cradled her belly as tears spilled down her face. She was drenched with sweat. It felt like she'd strained half the muscles in her back, but no permanent damage had been done. She collapsed on the bed, limp and spent, and she didn't move until the wail of an approaching siren shook her from her doze. The ambulance. She'd forgotten all about it.

Trembling from her exertions, she

got to her feet and made her way to the door.

Getting rid of the paramedics proved more difficult than she had anticipated, but she finally managed to persuade them that the emergency – whatever it was – had passed. She knew her baby was fine now and he didn't want to be poked and prodded in hospital any more than she did.

The paramedics exchanged a look and urged her to take advantage of the fact that they were there now, to let them run her in as a precaution, if nothing else. What did she have to lose?

But Molly refused to give in to their well-meaning pressure. She apologised for wasting their time and politely but firmly insisted that it was a false alarm.

Her behaviour surprised even her. It was as though she were watching the scene from afar, as though someone else were speaking through her. In the back of her mind was the desire to go with them to the hospital, to have whatever tests were needed to make sure the baby was fine. But another part of her, a stronger part, convinced her to send the ambulance away.

When she finally said good night to them she closed and locked the door, sagging against it with a sigh of relief. She felt like she'd got away with a crime.

Her son drifted softly in the goldfish bowl of her womb and she knew that he was sleeping. He twitched peacefully, like a dog dreaming of chasing rabbits. Molly dragged herself back to bed. The luminous moon bathed her in light as she fell into a deep and dreamless sleep.

❯

Morning brought clarity. And pain.

Molly cried out as she sat up in bed, her back a cluster of knots and her stomach feeling pummelled. The pain crushed any hope that the previous night's episode had been a dream.

But worse than the physical discomfort was the sudden awareness of her past behaviour. She'd treated Alice horribly. And Mark – she didn't know if she'd ever be able to face him again. What had got into her? Pregnancy made you a bit nuts; that much she knew. But surely this was extreme. Surely it couldn't all be blamed on hormones.

Even as she nudged closer to the thought that there was something wrong with her after all, she could feel the baby's resistance to the idea. It was the same resistance that had made her send the paramedics away, the same weird instinct to hide. It was like she'd gone feral, reverted to some primal urge to attack anyone who came near her.

Except it wasn't instinct, was it? The urge didn't come from her; it came from the baby.

She could feel him quivering inside with disapproval. It wasn't a voice as such, but the baby nonetheless spoke to her. He told her things. He listened to her thoughts. He controlled and directed her behaviour. But Molly was certain that last night he had been the one out of control.

No. None of this was remotely normal.

She hobbled into the bathroom and swallowed some paracetamol. Then she stared hard into the mirror and announced her intentions. "I'm going to call Alice and patch things up. And then I'm going to see a doctor." In a less confident voice she added "And you're not going to stop me."

The baby seethed at her treachery, growling in her mind like a mad dog trapped behind a fence. But his power had waned since last night's attack. Molly was in control now. Things were going to change.

●

Over the following days she set about repairing the damage she had done. Alice burst into tears and clung to her like a long lost sister. She understood, she forgave, she was overjoyed to have her friend back. Molly finally managed to prise her away and Alice extracted the promise that it wouldn't happen again.

Molly cringed, feeling like a wife beater. It wouldn't happen again. She promised.

The next step was easier. She lucked

into an appointment with an obstetrician who had a cancellation that afternoon, saving her days of anxious waiting and worrying. He examined her and found nothing wrong.

"All new mothers have these kinds of worries," Dr Tremayne told her, smiling. "Especially if it's your first child." He was old enough to convey authority and inspire confidence that he knew what he was talking about. It was obvious that he thought Molly had exaggerated her account of the strange attack but she felt reassured by him in spite of that.

"I thought I was going crazy," she said. "It was like the baby was talking to me, even controlling me."

Dr Tremayne nodded with a

heard-it-all-before smile. "Lots of women report a similar sense of communion. Some even feel it at the moment of conception. It's a powerful bond and it can be very scary indeed. Just because it isn't fully understood doesn't mean it isn't real."

She left his office feeling better than she had in weeks. She wasn't crazy at all. Armed with that knowledge she felt prepared for anything. Ignoring the baby's nervous trembling, she submitted to a blood test. The nurse told her the results would be back in a few days and in the interim she arranged an appointment for an ultrasound. She wanted to see her baby.

Molly lay on her back in the darkened room, her dress hitched up to expose her swollen belly. In spite of her newfound confidence she still felt oddly furtive, as though she were doing this behind someone's back.

The ultrasound technician was a fresh-faced northern lad named Greg who looked like he was barely out of school. Molly supposed it was her motherhood-to-be that made her suddenly feel so much older than everyone else. Whatever it was, she told herself, she'd just have to get used to it.

Greg squeezed a glob of lubricant onto the probe and smeared it around before pressing the device against Molly's belly. She peered anxiously at the screen where a spray of cloudy white appeared like a

48

spotlight. The image blurred and swam as Greg slid the probe across her taut skin. Then he held it still and Molly waited for the picture to make sense.

"There's your baby," he said cheerfully.

A series of jagged black lines formed shapes and shadows that could be transmissions from Mars for all she could make them out. "Where?"

"Just there. See his head?" He indicated a white curve on the left of the screen. "And it looks like – yes, you were right. It's a boy."

"Is he OK?"

He moved the probe around, peering at the screen and punching the keypad at intervals as the image melted and morphed into weird alien shapes.

Gradually the details of the foetus became clear: his bent knees, his rib cage, his tiny fluttering heart. He was curled tightly into a ball, his knees almost touching the top of his head.

"That's odd," Greg murmured.

"What is?"

When he didn't respond she knew he hadn't meant to say it aloud.

"What's odd? Tell me."

He pursed his lips and then pointed reluctantly to an area of the screen by the baby's head. "This shadow," he said, musing. "Of course, it *could* just be interference…"

Molly stiffened, hearing the unspoken "but". She held her breath as she waited for him to continue.

"How far along did you say you were?" he asked.

"I didn't. But I think it's been about three months."

He shook his head. "No way. Your baby's a lot older than that."

Molly stared at the picture, feeling helpless. The whole procedure was baffling to her. Whatever the scan was telling Greg couldn't be good news.

"I guess it's possible he's just got his hands in a funny position in front of his... face."

She heard the word *snout* as clearly as if he had spoken and her eyes filled with tears. "Is he deformed? Tell me."

"I don't think so," Greg said carefully. But again Molly could hear his uncertainty, sense the anxiety within him that he couldn't make sense of the image.

"Then what is it?"

Greg was hunched over the screen, staring intently at the amorphous mass that was her baby. "Do you see how cramped he is? It's almost like he's too big for the space he's in."

"But he's healthy?"

"He seems to be. But he's far too developed to be only three months old. You'll have to wait for the results of the blood test to determine how old he really is. I just don't understand that shadow."

He was silent for a long time, moving the probe slowly back and forth and shaking his head in confusion at the signals it transmitted. He was like a student puzzling over a difficult exam question. Molly intercepted his thoughts: he was thinking about dogs for some reason. His mind wasn't on the job at all. The baby jerked angrily, as though irritated by the attention and Molly felt the frustration along with him.

Finally she snapped. "Are you sure you know what you're doing?"

Greg stared at her in the darkness and she smelled the same fear on him that she'd smelled on Mark. Fear of *her*.

"Of course," he said, but she heard the shakiness in his voice. No. He clearly *didn't* know what he was doing. He was just a kid, for god's sake. He'd probably only been taught how to use the machine the day before. Her worry evaporated in the light of his obvious inexperience.

He pressed the probe against her belly again as though desperate to prove her wrong but Molly pushed him away and shuffled to her feet. "I think that's enough," she said. "My son's fine. That's all I need to know." She tore a strip of paper off the couch and scrubbed away the lubricant on her belly.

Greg moved aside for her and stood by the wall like a teenager spurned at a dance. "Er… do you want a photo?" he asked, then added awkwardly, "Most women do."

Molly glanced at the sign taped to the door and laughed. "For a fiver? No thanks. I think I'll wait until I can take my own pictures." She thanked him breezily as she swept out of the room, closing the door behind her.

Alice looked up with a smile from the waiting room, setting aside an ancient copy of *Marie Claire*. "Well?" she asked excitedly. "How'd it go?"

"The baby's fine. Perfectly healthy. And my sixth sense was right; it's a boy."

Alice hopped in place and clapped her hands together like a little girl. "That's brilliant! Oh, I'm so relieved."

"*You're* relieved?" Molly laughed. "Here I was thinking I'd been raped by an alien."

A young woman looked up with a scowl at that and put a protective arm around the scruffy toddler beside her.

Alice rolled her eyes. "Let's get out of

here. Come on. Dinner's on me. You want pizza?"

"No," Molly said, considering. "Steak. I really fancy a big juicy steak."

The results of the blood test came back a few days later. Everything was perfectly normal. She was beginning to love the sound of that word.

When the knifing cramps returned, Molly again felt the baby's terror and desperation. It had been almost a month since the first episode and she'd put it from her mind completely. Now it was happening again.

The baby writhed and contorted in pain

and she was helpless to do anything but be the voice of his screams.

She reached for the phone but then yanked her hand away as though burned. The baby was pleading with her again. Pleading for secrecy, for complicity. Molly felt herself falling under his spell, just as she had before. She did not try to resist. Instead she curled herself into a ball and bit down on the pillow to stifle her cries. She didn't want the neighbours ringing the police.

Time passed in a blinding haze of agony and Molly abandoned herself to it. The moon danced in the black sky, teasing and tormenting. Molly felt oddly connected to it, as though it were pulling at her, moulding her as it did the tides.

From deep inside her womb came a faint but chilling howl and Molly found herself howling along with it.

●

The light had changed. The sun's incandescent glare threatened to blind her and she shielded her eyes as she crept into the bathroom to be sick. Her morning ritual. Her head was pounding and her body ached as though she'd spent the night on the rack in some mediaeval dungeon.

She couldn't remember ever feeling this wretched and it took some time for the fog to clear. Then the baby stirred and she flashed back to the night before. The attack, the episode, whatever it was.

Her son's unyielding insistence that she ride out the storm.

Since speaking to Dr Tremayne Molly had fully accepted and embraced the communion she felt with her baby, questioning neither his needs nor his strange cravings. But last night frightened her. They had both been in terrible pain, even worse than before, but Molly found she could not remember much of the ordeal.

Her body had clearly been through it and at first she supposed it was a mercy she had blanked it out. She was no stranger to waking with holes in her memory, but this was different. It only took her a moment to recognise the baby's subtle mesmerism: she couldn't remember because he didn't *want* her to remember.

She recalled the heightened clarity she'd had after the first episode, the sense that, while the baby might be fine, she most assuredly was not. That feeling was even stronger now. Whatever the tests showed, whatever Dr Tremayne had said, there was something wrong. She needed help.

Her insides clenched as the baby showed his displeasure at her train of thought. It was almost like he was pacing around in there, growling and snapping whenever Molly went against his wishes. She winced and took a deep breath as she waited for the pain to subside.

"No," she hissed, gritting her teeth. "I'm calling Alice."

She fought her way to the phone and smiled at her petty victory. The baby could kick and protest all he wanted; she still had control of her body. And it *was* hers, not his.

A little while later Alice arrived looking alarmed and flustered. "What happened? What's wrong?" She glanced down at Molly's belly. "Is it the baby?"

Molly pulled Alice down beside her on the couch. "I have to tell you something and it's going to sound crazy. But there's no one else I can talk to about it."

"I'm listening."

Molly took a deep breath and let it out slowly. "I think there's something wrong with the baby." At Alice's look of dismay she quickly pressed on, wanting to get it out before she lost her nerve. Or before she was silenced. "Sometimes I can't help but wonder if the baby isn't – well, if it isn't human."

Alice's hand drifted to her mouth and Molly intercepted a series of abstract fears as they flashed through her friend's mind: infanticide, prison, padded cell.

"I don't know how much longer I'll have control of my thoughts so I have to say this now. There's so much I haven't told you and I know it sounds crazy but you have to believe me. I can sense what the baby's thinking and feeling. More than that – I can sense what other people are thinking. I can smell their fear. But mostly it's the baby. I feel like he's been controlling me, making me keep him a secret. Something happened last night – something that happened before – and he kept me from calling for help."

A vicious cramp suddenly seized her and she gasped. "It's him," she said, forcing the words out through the pain. "This is what he does. He's afraid."

"Afraid? Of what?"

"I don't know. This happened once before. He was like this all day and then, at night—" She whimpered as another spasm hit her. "I was in so much pain I called an ambulance but then suddenly I was fine."

Alice gasped. "You called an ambulance?"

"Yeah, but I sent it away. I thought I was having a miscarriage but then just like that it was over." She winced again as the baby struggled inside.

"When was this? Why didn't you tell me?"

"Last month. I didn't think it was a big deal so I just—"

"What are you talking about? It sounds like a *very* big deal!"

"The baby didn't want me to go."

Alice looked horrified.

"I know how it sounds," Molly said, hanging her head in misery. "But it happened again last night—"

"Jesus!"

"—and he wouldn't let me call. But like before, I was fine this morning. Only I can feel him getting angry at what I'm telling you. He's fighting me. But he's also very afraid of something and I have no idea what."

Alice stared at her in blank-faced astonishment. When she spoke it was with forced optimism. "But didn't the doctor say all those crazy thoughts were normal?"

"Yes and no," Molly said. "I didn't really give him the full picture. I think maybe I wasn't allowed to."

"But the blood test… The ultrasound… You said everything was fine."

"I know. But maybe he can control those things so he *seems* normal."

Even as she said it, Molly knew how delusional it all sounded. And the horror and dismay on Alice's face only reinforced it. Still, she had to express her greatest fear, had to get it out. Molly met Alice's eyes as she said the mutinous words. "I think he's evil."

Alice shook her head violently, rejecting the madness of the idea. "Do you realise how crazy that sounds?"

Molly gave a harsh little laugh. "Believe me, I know exactly how crazy it sounds. What's more, I know the *baby* knows how crazy it sounds. That's why he doesn't want any doctors getting their hands on me. Or him."

She gritted her teeth against another cramp, the baby's response to her treachery.

"See?" she hissed. "He doesn't want me talking to you."

Alice's eyes filled with tears. She stared at her friend in profound dismay and Molly tried not to eavesdrop on her thoughts. They were the same ones she'd have if their positions were reversed.

"I have to get rid of it," Molly said.

At that, the baby gave her a powerful kick and she clutched her abdomen.

Alice took Molly by the arms and made her look her in the eyes. "Molly, listen to me. I don't want you to do anything rash. I think you should talk to the doctor again. Tell him exactly what you told me and see what he says."

"He won't believe me."

"He will," Alice said firmly. "And he'll be able to help you. Didn't he say the crazy thoughts might get worse?"

He certainly did tell her that. He'd shared a couple of anecdotes with her that had made her blood run cold. One woman had blinded herself with a screwdriver, convinced that her baby was seeing through her eyes and spying for its father, who she'd run away from. Another believed that the baby inside her was dead, that the illusion of kicking was simply the worms devouring its corpse.

The accounts had put Molly's fears into perspective. Her own worries seemed trivial by comparison. Now here she was telling Alice her baby was evil, that it wasn't human. Could it really just be all in her mind? She cast about for something to say and came up with nothing.

Alice seized the moment. "Please call

the doctor. Tell him everything and if he thinks what you're saying is rational I'll help you do whatever's necessary."

Molly relented. "OK, you win. His number's on the fridge."

●

The next day she was back in Dr Tremayne's office.

His forehead creased with concern as she made her confession, but, like Alice, he reminded her that the physical evidence was against her. Even the strange attacks could be explained away by hormones or anxiety, what he called "conversion" symptoms. There was clearly an underlying psychological explanation for everything she had told him.

"What does worry me – only slightly, you understand – is this conviction of yours that the baby is controlling your thoughts and behaviour and that he can influence test results."

"I googled schizophrenia, Doctor. That's only one symptom."

He looked startled.

Yes, she'd plucked the word straight from his mind. But even if she told him that, he'd only see it as a conjuror's trick. He'd have a logical explanation for it. However, she didn't have the courage to voice the other word floating around in his thoughts: Sectioning. Just in case he was right.

"I don't want to worry you, Molly, but the things you're describing are a bit beyond my remit. I'd like you to talk to a friend of mine."

"A psychiatrist," she said, crestfallen. She had pinned her hopes on him being able to dismiss her concerns as easily as he had before.

"He's a good listener," Dr Tremayne said, "and he has a lot of experience with this kind of thing."

Molly thought of the woman who had blinded herself and wondered what "kind of thing" *she'd* had. "OK," she said, taking the proffered slip of paper.

His name was Dr McCulloch and he was a tweedy academic type in a drab brown suit that perfectly complemented his bored countenance. His bushy grey eyebrows seemed to weigh his face down, making eye contact almost impossible. But he managed to engineer a smile (of a sort) for her and she ignored the restless movements of the baby as she sank into the comfortable chair he offered her.

"Not human," he mused, looking down at the notes he'd been scribbling throughout her recitation of events. He seemed mildly intrigued, like a bug collector who'd just found an unfamiliar specimen.

"Well, sometimes he is and sometimes he isn't," Molly clarified. "I know it sounds crazy but he's not evil all the time. What I mean is – there are times when I feel him invading my mind, making me do things I don't want to—"

"Like sending the paramedics away."

"Yes. And at other times I genuinely love him and we have this intense bond. I feel his pain and fear."

"And you can read minds."

She winced at his choice of words. "Not 'read minds' as such. I can sense feelings and occasionally words. It's more a vague impression of certain thoughts."

He looked up from his notes with another hint of a smile. "Can you tell me what I'm thinking right now?"

Molly blushed, feeling foolish. "No," she admitted. "The emotions have to be strong – like fear or desire."

"I see." He sat back in his chair and regarded her solemnly. "Well, Miss

Landon—"

"Landor."

"Miss Landor. The idea that a baby wants to take over your life is a perfectly natural fear. Certainly not just a persecutory delusion. A baby *will* take over your life. It's hardly surprising that you might perceive such a traumatic change as evil, given the carefree lifestyle you say you used to lead."

Molly looked down at the floor, abashed. "Carefree" was putting it mildly.

"But some of the more, shall we say, schizophrenic symptoms – to use your word – those are the ones that need watching. Pre-natal psychosis is rare but not unheard of. Still, I'm reluctant to leap to that conclusion in your case, since there are so many other more likely factors at work here."

It was what she had both hoped for and dreaded. It was all in her mind. The idea would have reassured her were it not for the undeniable fact that she *knew* there was more going on inside her than any of these so-called experts could possibly put a name to. At the same time, she was fully aware of how paranoid that "undeniable fact" was. She believed this crazy thing in spite of all objective evidence to the contrary. So either she was right and there was something evil inside her and no one would believe her – or she was mad.

"Under the circumstances," she said gravely, "I think I prefer being mad."

Dr McCulloch grumbled that "mad" was a melodramatic word and that she shouldn't stigmatise herself or her perfectly normal and natural fears.

She resisted the urge to tell him that she could always wring its neck if it proved her right in the delivery room.

●

Alice did her best to reinforce Dr McCulloch's temporary madness theory and over the days that followed, Molly found herself subscribing to it more and more.

Whatever weird feelings she might have had were fading with time and she once more swelled with love for the baby.

She murmured to him at night, played him music, sang to him and promised him the world. How could she ever have thought such terrible things about him?

Although the blood test had confirmed that she was only about four months pregnant, she looked much further advanced than that. Again Dr Tremayne had told her it was nothing to be concerned about. The foetus was bigger than most but he wasn't worried. It might mean a more painful birth, but Molly said she was prepared for that.

A week later she was curled up beside Alice on the sofa watching a film when the baby began to panic. She cried out, clutching her belly.

Alice was instantly alarmed. "What is

it? Molly, are you OK? What's wrong?"

Molly's eyes filled with tears. Instinct battled instinct and she realised she had been tricked again. Love turned to terror as the creature inside resumed its frantic contortions, scrambling painfully inside her. It was happening again.

"Help me," she moaned. "I was right all along. It wants to kill me!" She buried her face in the cushions as the baby began another assault on her womb.

Alice shouted something but Molly couldn't make out the words. The baby was screaming inside her and the pain was worse than ever. She felt it building like a sneeze, like an orgasm, and with a jolt of lucidity she suddenly knew who the father was.

The guy she'd met at Glastonbury. Mr Rough Stuff. The one who'd given her the best orgasm of her life but left her bruised and scratched and sore for days after. Ah yes, she remembered now. And his progeny had done the same thing. Seduced her, used her. It didn't love her. It never had.

"Please help me," she whimpered. "I have to get rid of it. You have to take me to the hospital."

As she spoke she felt the frenzied hammering of the baby's heart. Something was coming, something terrible.

"Come on," Alice said, pulling Molly to her feet. "I can get us there in ten minutes."

As the car pulled away from the kerb with a screech Molly peered up through the windscreen. Clouds drifted like a veil across the staring eye of the moon.

"They say there are more births on the full moon than any other night," she mused.

"And murders," Alice said darkly. She switched on the headlights and sent the car out into traffic, where she ran the first of many red lights.

Alice talked to the triage nurse while Molly staggered to a chair, her arms wrapped round her belly as though it might burst.

A man sat opposite her, clutching a blood-soaked tea towel to his leg. The smell was overpowering, so ripe she could taste it. Her mouth flooded with saliva and she swallowed it down. How could the others around her stand it? In her distress the smell became an unbearable noise, like the relentless pounding of a pneumatic drill. She sank to her knees on the floor, wrapping her arms over her head as she tried to block her hideously acute senses. The baby raged inside her. Soon the pain would consume him and Molly along with it, just as it had before.

No sooner had the realisation dawned than the knifing cramps struck her with the force of a thunderbolt. Molly screamed and doubled over as much as her distended body would allow, convinced that she was being wrenched inside-out.

Voices swam out of the madness of pain and suddenly there were hands all around her, pushing, pulling, grabbing.

"Get it out of me!" Molly cried. "It's not human!"

Then something soft was pressing against her back and she realised that she was lying down. There was the slap of many feet on the floor as she was wheeled rapidly down a corridor and into a room. She screamed again as another wave of agony pulled her under and someone was murmuring in her ear, telling her to calm down, to breathe. A pair of strong arms held her down.

"You're safe. We've got you."

Something cold and wet pressed against her belly and she heard a collective gasp. Then a man's voice said "Oh my god."

"What the hell is that?" someone else asked, the voice pitched so high with disbelief Molly couldn't tell if it was male or female.

Panting for breath, she craned round to see what they were looking at. On the screen was the familiar white spray of the ultrasound transmission. And floating in the murky grey sea was her baby. The pale figure jerked violently, arching its back and lashing what could only be a tail. But the real horror was at the other end, where the round bulb of its head was stretching and elongating into a canine snout.

A woman screamed and there was a

crash as metal objects went clattering to the floor. A door opened and footsteps raced away down the corridor.

Then the image vanished and someone shouted "Simon!" The man nearest her gaped at the others before ducking down to retrieve the probe he had dropped. With shaking hands he pressed it against Molly's belly again and the group watched as the figure contorted further, its every movement clearly an agony. Its tiny limbs thinned and lengthened and for a moment Molly forgot her own pain as she stared at the screen, transfixed.

Inside her, something was being born. But it was no miracle; it was an abomination. The creature threw back its head as a pair of tapered wolf ears

sprouted from its skull and the room
fell silent as it began to howl, the wild,
full-throated freezing howl of a wolf.
The ghostly silhouette clambered onto
all fours and lifted its head, looking up.
Then it began scrabbling and raking its
claws against the walls of its prison,
desperate to escape.

The pain was beyond anything Molly
had ever imagined, but it got worse
when the tiny wolf sank its fangs into the
lining of her womb and began to chew its
way out.

The lights came on and the room was
a flurry of activity, with raised voices
and frantic movement. Shapes flowed
around her like water and she felt herself
fading. Colours spun before her eyes and
she suddenly longed to see the moon,

to embrace its unearthly glow again. But the moon was far away, out of sight, out of reach. It had abandoned her. She had served a purpose but she could have no part beyond it. The creature inside her had one single desire: life. Life at any cost, even if it meant her death.

There was a deep wet ripping and then ropes of blood leapt in the sterile light of the room. A pair of thin furry arms parted the skin of her belly like a curtain and a blood-soaked muzzle emerged, baring its teeth in a lupine smile. She met its eyes and for a moment she held its gleaming yellow gaze. Hatred turned to love as she saw at last the creature her body had nurtured. She lifted one hand weakly to stroke its sleek wet fur.

Then it leapt free of her and all was chaos. A man loosed an anguished scream. Something large crashed to the floor. An alarm sounded. People fled like panicked sheep, shouting for help. Outside in the corridor she could hear Alice calling her name, could taste her fear as she caught sight of the wolf and turned to run. She wouldn't be fast enough.

Molly's eyes closed with the bliss of strange revelation. The wolf's father hadn't deigned to bite her, to make her like him. But the baby had. Her torn flesh tingled as it began knitting itself back together. A single dedicated nurse had stayed with her and Molly grinned as the woman's eyes widened with the impossibility of what she had seen and was seeing now. They would widen even more when Molly began her own transformation. The moon was calling her.

About the Author

Thana Niveau is a horror and science fiction writer. She is the author of the short story collections *Octoberland*, *Unquiet Waters*, and *From Hell to Eternity*, as well as the novel *House of Frozen Screams*. She has been shortlisted three times for the British Fantasy Awards – for *Octoberland* and *From Hell to Eternity*, and for her short story *Death Walks En Pointe*.

She shares her life with fellow writer

John Llewellyn Probert, in a crumbling gothic tower filled with arcane books and curiosities. And toy dinosaurs.

Also by Thana Niveau

Octoberland,

Unquiet Waters

From Hell to Eternity

House of Frozen Screams

… and more.

We would like to thank everyone who made this project possible,
via the Kickstarter and outside of it.

Specific thanks goes to:

Aaron Armitage

David Parker

Ross Warren

More dyslexic friendly

titles coming soon...

BOTH
PUBLISHING